MERMIN™
BOOK FIVE: MAKING WAVES
KING MERUS
QUEEN BLU
MERMA
OMER
MAK

MERMIN™

BOOK FIVE: MAKING WAVES

Written and illustrated by
Joey Weiser

Colored by
Joey Weiser and Michele Chidester

Edited by
Robin Herrera

Designed by
Keith Wood
with
Angie Knowles

Published by Oni Press, Inc.

founder & chief financial officer, Joe Nozemack
publisher, James Lucas Jones
v.p. of creative & business development, Charlie Chu
director of operations, Brad Rooks
director of publicity, Melissa Meszaros
director of sales, Margot Wood
marketing manager, Rachel Reed
special projects manager, Amber O'Neill
director of design & production, Troy Look
graphic designer, Hilary Thompson
junior graphic designer, Kate Z. Stone
junior graphic designer, Sonja Synak
digital prepress lead, Angie Knowles
executive editor, Ari Yarwood
senior editor, Robin Herrera
associate editor, Desiree Wilson
administrative assistant, Alissa Sallah
logistics associate, Jung Lee
warehouse assistant, Scott Sharkey

onipress.com
facebook.com/onipress
twitter.com/onipress
onipress.tumblr.com
instagram.com/onipress
tragic-planet.com

First Edition: August 2018

ISBN 978-1-62010-523-8
eISBN 978-1-62010-395-1

Printed in China.

Library of Congress Control Number: 2016917152
1 2 3 4 5 6 7 8 9 10

MANY TIDES AGO, THE PEOPLE OF THE SEA LIVED AMONGST THE OTHER CREATURES AT THE OCEAN'S FLOOR.

THE SEA GRANTED ONE OF THE ANCIENT SEA PEOPLE POWER OVER HER, AND HE BECAME THE FIRST KING.

THIS POWER IS PASSED THROUGH GENERATIONS OF THE ROYAL FAMILY, AND WITH IT THEY RULE OVER THE UNDERSEA REALM.

THIS WAS THE WAY FOR AGES, WHEN NEW PEOPLE FROM THE SURFACE ARRIVED.

THESE "HUMANS" WERE MORE SCIENTIFICALLY ADVANCED THAN THEIR FELLOW SURFACE-DWELLERS AND CAME TO THE SEA FOR ESCAPE FROM THE BARBARISM ABOVE.

THE PEOPLE OF THE SEA SHARED THEIR KNOWLEDGE OF THE DEPTHS, LIKE THE MYSTERIOUSLY POWERFUL ENERGEODES, AND THE SURFACE HUMANS SHARED THEIR TECHNOLOGY.

AND SO, TWO KINGDOMS AROSE AT THE BOTTOM OF THE SEA.

MER-PEOPLE ADOPTED THE ATLANTEAN WAY OF LIFE, FINDING CONVENIENCE IN LIVING IN DRY SPACES.

BOTH KINGDOMS FLOURISHED AS THEY LEARNED TO USE ENERGEODES TO POWER THEIR CITIES.

GENERATIONS PASSED AS THEY SHARED THE OCEAN FLOOR.

HOWEVER, ENERGEODES HAVE BECOME MORE SCARCE, AND TENSION OVER MINING TERRITORIES HAS RISEN.

ATLANTIS AND MER EVENTUALLY MADE CLEAR DISTINCTIONS OF WHICH AREAS WITH KNOWN ENERGEODE MINES BELONGED TO EACH KINGDOM. BUT THERE IS STILL MUCH OF THE SEA FLOOR LEFT UNCLEAR WHO HAS CLAIM TO IT!
DESPITE LIVING IN RELATIVE PEACE FOR AGES, IT SEEMS THAT THE WAVE OF WAR IS ABOUT TO CRASH...

CHAPTER
ONE

...AND SO YOU SEE, MERMIN...
...OUR PEOPLE WERE BESTOWED THE RIGHT TO THE OCEAN BY THE SEA HERSELF!
YEAH, I'VE GONE OVER THIS STUFF WITH MY INSTRUCTOR...
...IT'S JUST HARD TO BELIEVE...
...WE'RE ACTUALLY ON OUR WAY TO WAR!
WE ARE ON OUR WAY TO ATLANTIS TO RESCUE YOUR HUMAN FRIEND!
YEAH, I GUESS...
...I'M NOT SURE A WHOLE WAR PARTY IS NECESSARY...

ATLANTIS HAS BEEN PRACTICALLY BEGGING FOR WAR!
THEY'VE BEEN PUSHING THE BOUNDARIES FOR SOME TIME, AND YOUR BROTHER OMER VALIANTLY PERISHED IN BATTLE OVER IT!!!
NOW THIS?!?
MERMIN, YOU WILL BE BY MY SIDE AS WE RECLAIM WHAT IS RIGHTFULLY OURS!
(sigh... now i'm remembering why i ran away...)

HOW'S YOUR HELMET, BENNI?
A-A LITTLE BIG...
B-BUT I'LL, uh, MANAGE... YOUR OXYGEN TANK I-IS WORKING AND EVERYTHING...?
YUP! SEEMS TO BE!
BOY, I HOPE WE CAN FIND PETE!!
DON'T WORRY, GUYS!
WE GOT THIS!
TOO LATE TO TURN BACK...!

...ALMOST THE ENTIRE ARMY HAS LEFT MER ALREADY!
JUST PUT IT ON, RANDY!!

AFTER WE LEAVE THE AIRLOCK, WATER IS GONNA FILL THE LOCKER!

WHY WOULD THEY EVEN MAKE IT LIKE THAT?!
VENTILATION IS VERY IMPORTANT. IT PREVENTS MOLD.
NOW, PUT YOUR HELMET ON!
VRRRMMMMMM
SSHHKK!
SOUNDS LIKE WE'RE IN THE AIRLOCK!
...oh no...

WHAT?!
WHAT?!?
I... I JUST REALIZED! HUMANS ALSO NEED AN AIR TANK TO BREATHE UNDERWATER!
ACK! HERE COMES THE WATER!
THAT'S IT! I'M OUTTA HERE!!
LET ME BACK IN!!!
BANG! BANG!
HOLD ON! YOU HAVE SOME TIME BEFORE YOU RUN OUT OF AIR!
uh...
THERE!!

WHA--?
THOSE SHIPS HAVE AIR IN THEM!
COME ON!!

HANG ON, RANDY!!
ALMOST THERE...!
SPLAT!

HUH?!?

WELCOME TO "THE DUMPLING"!
CAPTAIN, A-ARE YOU SURE THIS...VESSEL... IS SEAWORTHY?
OH, YES! SHE'S STATE-OF-THE-ART!
(for the time she was made)

POP!
uh...IT'S SUPPOSED TO DO THAT.
LISTEN... YOU'VE PAID FOR ME TO FIND YOUR CHILDREN...
...AND THAT'S WHAT I SHALL DO!
MY TEAM HAS BEEN RESEARCHING ODD SIGNALS FROM BELOW...
YES...

IF, IN FACT, THEY'VE BEEN TAKEN TO AN UNDERSEA CITY, WE HAVE A THEORY OF WHERE WE MAY FIND THEM.
...AND THEIR LITTLE GREEN FRIEND...
mutter mutter
DID THAT SEEM... WEIRD?
DID WE TELL THEM THAT MERMIN IS GREEN...?
SIGH
THIS WHOLE ENDEAVOR MAKES MY STOMACH HURT...

NO TIME FOR SEASICKNESS, CREW!
clap!
IT'S TIME TO DEPART!
AYE! AYE!

DIVE!
TO THE GREAT UNKNOWN WE GO!!

CHAPTER
TWO

WE STILL HEADING IN THE RIGHT DIRECTION?
I... THINK SO...

YOU "THINK" SO?!
LOOK... THE TUNNELS UNDER ATLANTIS ARE COMPLICATED!
WITHOUT THAT MAP ALEXIS COPIED FOR US, WE MIGHT NOT'VE MADE IT OUT AT ALL!
COURTESY OF OUR LOCAL LIBRARY!
BRINGING US FOOD AND SUPPLIES... VISITING US NIGHT AFTER NIGHT...
...I'M HAPPY TO HAVE HER ALONG.
SHE CAN BE TRUSTED!

HOW WAS IT THAT YOU GOT THE KEYS TO OUR CELL, ALEXIS?
IT WAS EASY! THERE WERE HARDLY ANY GUARDS TONIGHT!
HMMM...
SEEMS TOO EASY...
COULD WE BE FOLLOWED?
DO YOU KNOW ANYTHING ABOUT THAT, PEAT?
WHAT?! NO!
VERY SUSPICIOUS!
YOU TELL ANYONE ABOUT OUR ESCAPE, PEAT?!
HUH?!?
LAY OFF, GUYS!

I-I TOLD YOU... I'M NOT FROM ATLANTIS!
YOU'RE FROM "DRY LAND"?! YOU EXPECT US TO BELIEVE THAT?!?
sniff EVERY AFTERNOON I'D WATCH THE PADLOCK BUSTER/MAXIMAN POWER BLOCK ON ZTV... THEN TOBY AND I WOULD PRETEND TO HAVE OUR OWN ADVENTURES...
...WELL, NOW I AM HAVING A REAL ADVENTURE!
IT... IT WAS EXCITING AT FIRST, TO VISIT MER...
...BUT NOW I DON'T KNOW IF I'LL EVER SEE MY FRIENDS OR FAMILY AGAIN!! sniff

PEAT... I DON'T KNOW WHAT "BAD LUCK LOBSTER" IS, BUT I BELIEVE YOU.
Tch! WE DON'T HAVE TIME FOR THIS.
SO... HOW IS MERMIN THESE DAYS?
MERMIN'S GREAT...
I MEAN... HE WAS WHEN WE WERE ON DRY LAND...

HE WAS SO FUN AND EXCITED TO BE WITH US...
E-EVEN THOUGH I DIDN'T KNOW WHAT TO DO WITH THIS FISH-BOY... I WAS HAPPY TO BE WITH HIM...
BUT IT'S BEEN DIFFERENT SINCE WE GOT TO MER. THINGS ARE TENSE WITH HIS... YOUR DAD...
...HE DOESN'T SMILE AS MUCH...
OKAY.
LET'S GET MOVING...

LET'S PUT A SMILE ON MERMIN'S FACE.

MY CREW AND I, HERE, WERE SENT OUT BY MY FATHER, KING MERUS, TO SCOUT FOR UNCLAIMED LAND RICH WITH ENERGEODES.
BUT ATLANTIS IS LOOKING FOR THIS AS WELL...
WE ENCOUNTERED AN ATLANTEAN CREW AND A FIGHT BROKE OUT!
WE COULD'VE HANDLED THEM, EASILY!
BUT THEY HAD REINFORCEMENTS HIDING ON THE OTHER SIDE OF THE MOUNTAIN!
BAH!

SO, WE WERE CAPTURED!
THEY DON'T KNOW I'M THE KING'S SON. SO, HOPEFULLY IT WON'T CAUSE BIG WAVES THAT WE WERE CAUGHT...
OR THAT WE'VE ESCAPED!
EVERYONE IN MER THINKS THAT YOU'RE DEAD!
Hm.
THEN WE SHOULD GET HOME AS SOON AS POSSIBLE!
MY FATHER'S TEMPER...
ESPECIALLY WHEN ATLANTIS IS INVOLVED...

OMER! THIS IS IT!
ALRIGHT, KIDS. PUT YOUR MASKS ON. THIS LEADS TO AN EXIT CHAMBER.
BLUB!
WOO-HOO!

AAHHH~! FRESH SEA WATER!!
WE MADE IT!
HEY! WHO IS THAT?!
Uh-Oh.
THE MER PRISONERS!!!
AND THAT HUMAN KID!!

ATLANTEAN SCOUTS!
YOU SLIMEY EEL!! THIS WAS A TRAP!!!
WHAT?! NO!!
YOU WON'T TAKE US BACK!!
VZZZZZ

HA!
OOF!
WHACK!
ARG!
AUH!
NGHAH!

STOP RIGHT THERE!!
I'VE GOT YOUR SHARK-TOOTHED SPY!
RGH! NO!!
SPY? THAT CRAZY CHILD WHO SAYS HE'S FROM DRY LAND?
HE...TOLD YOU THAT TOO...?

SIGH
WOAH!
WHOOSH!
SHOOOOOOo
LET PEAT DOWN AND TAKE CARE OF THIS.
RRRRR
SNAP!
THE ROYAL POWERS! WHO ARE YOU??
LISTEN... WE DON'T WANT TO HURT YOU.
WOooaahhhh

I PROMISE YOU, THESE KIDS ARE COMING WITH US VOLUNTARILY.
AND YOU ARE NOW UNARMED.
WE'RE LEAVING NOW.
PEACEFULLY.
HA!
DO YOU KNOW WHY IT WAS SO EASY TO ESCAPE, TODAY?!

MOST OF ATLANTIS'S MILITARY HAS LEFT!
THEY ARE ON THEIR WAY TO INVADE MER!!

CHAPTER
THREE

SIR, WE ARE ABOUT TO REACH THE HALFWAY POINT BETWEEN MER AND ATLANTIS...
SURELY, THIS SHOW OF STRENGTH WILL BRING MERUS OUT OF HIS HOLE!
AND I WILL DEMAND AN EXPLANATION FOR HIS CRIME! KIDNAPPING ATLANTEAN CHILDREN AND BRAIN-WASHING THEM?!
IT IS TRULY BAFFLING... I DO NOT SEE WHAT PURPOSE IT COULD POSSIBLY SERVE...
ALL OF OUR TROUBLES OVER THE ENERGEODE MINES, AND NOW THIS...
SIGH

SIR! A MER WAR-PARTY APPROACHES!
WHAT?!?
THEIR SCOUTS SPOTTED OURS, AND KING MERUS HAS REQUESTED PARLEY WITH YOU.
Y-YES. I AGREE.

GREETINGS, FROM KING GLAUCUS, RULER OF ATLANTIS!
THIS, ah, THIS VALLEY IS NEUTRAL GROUND, UNCLAIMED BY EITHER KINGDOM.
A GOOD, ah, PLACE TO MEET.
INDEED.

WHY HAVE YOU TAKEN YOUR ARMY OUT TO SEA, MERUS?
I WOULD LIKE TO ASK YOU THE SAME THING...
WELL... I ASKED FIRST!
WELL, I ASKED SECOND WHICH IS MORE RECENT! WHAT OF IT?!?!?
a-ah... SIR, PLEASE...
I HAVE SOME QUESTIONS FOR YOU, AND IT IS UNPLEASANT...
OH REALLY?
DOES IT HAVE ANYTHING TO DO WITH THE RESIDENT OF MY KINGDOM YOU ARE HOLDING CAPTIVE?!?

Oh...HE MAY BE REFERRING TO THE MER SCOUTING GROUP WHO RECENTLY ENCOUNTERED ONE OF OUR OWN...
THAT IS ANOTHER MATTER ENTIRELY THAT YOU DO NOT WANT TO GET INTO WITH ME RIGHT NOW...
W-WAIT...ah, WHAT ABOUT THAT, ah, SCOUTING CREW...?
THIS IS ALL BESIDES THE POINT!
YOU ARE KID-NAPPING ATLANTEAN CHILDREN!!!

THAT IS PREPOSTEROUS!
IS IT?
IS IT??
WE HAVE FIRSTHAND EVIDENCE THAT MER HAS BEEN ABDUCTING AND BRAINWASHING OUR CHILDREN!
FILLING THEIR MINDS WITH CRAZY IDEAS!!

WHAT AN ABSURD ACCUSATION!!
HUMAN KID WITH STRANGE IDEAS...?
OH NO! WHAT IF HE MEANS PETE?!
MOVE ASIDE, MERMIN. I'VE HEARD ALL I NEED!
D-DAD! WAIT!! I THINK--

IN THE NAME OF THE FORMER ROYAL HEIR, MY BELOVED SON, OMER...
I COMMAND THE GREAT MER FORCES...
w-wait...

ATTACK!!!
RAAAAAA
YAA

AAAAAAAH
AAA

TH-TH-THE P-PLAN WAS TO GO W-WITH THE ARMY AND THEN SPLIT OFF TO SNEAK INSIDE ATLANTIS TO FIND PETE!
I-I DON'T THINK EVEN KING MERUS WAS, uh, EXPECTING TO SEE THE A-ATLANTEAN FORCES!
VMMMM
RAGH!
POP!
HEY!!

WOAH!
WAY TO GO, SIS!
OKAY, KIDS...
are you... humans...?
WE'RE NOT REALLY IN THE ARMY...
BUT WE ARE REALLY IN THE MIDDLE OF THIS...
RAAAHH
YAAHHHH
...SO, UNTIL WE CAN FIND A SAFE PLACE...
OVER THERE!
GO, MEN!
...WE'VE GOT TO LOOK OUT FOR EACH OTHER!

VWOOO
SHAAAAHHHH
BOOM!
WHAT!! YOU GUYS HAVE LASERS?!?

BOTH SIDES HAVE DEVELOPED WAYS TO WEAPONIZE THE POWER OF ENERGEODES.
IT'S THE ONLY WAY THOSE WEAK HUMANS HAVE A CHANCE OF FIGHTING US!
HUMANS ARE SMART ENOUGH THAT WE RULE THE WORLD!
Heh!
WHOSE SIDE ARE YOU ON?!
QUIET BACK THERE!! I'M TRYING TO KEEP US ALIVE IN HERE!!!

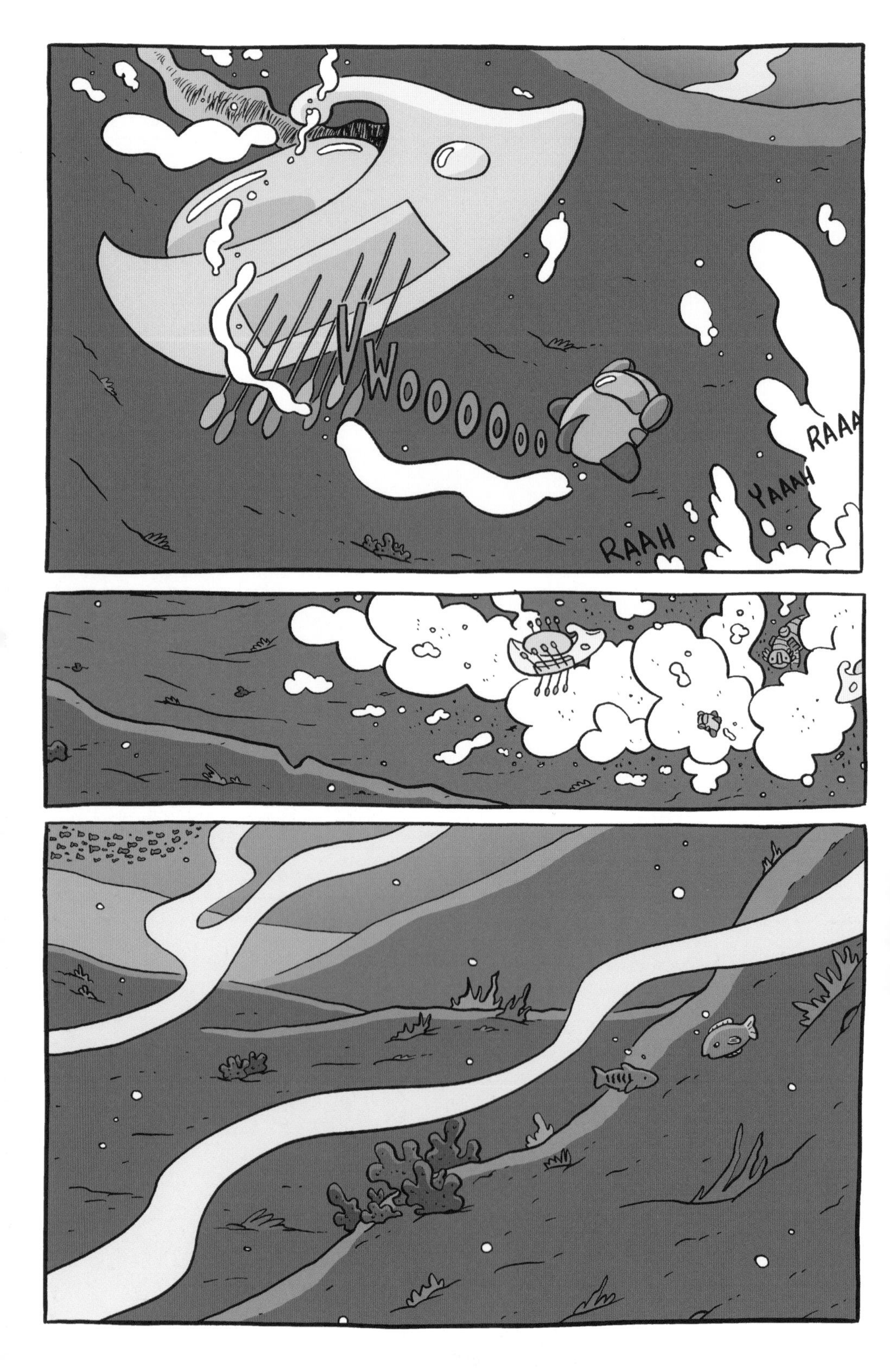
VWOOOOOoo
RAAA
YAAAH
RAAH

LOOKS LIKE WE'RE SAFELY OUTSIDE OF ATLANTEAN BORDERS...
GOOD.
THANKS FOR THE RIDE!
OF COURSE...
YOU COULD NEVER SWIM AS FAST AS US! HA HA

AND YOU HEARD THOSE SCOUTS!
SO, DO WE ALL TRUST PEAT NOW?
YES.
ALL OF US??

YES.
GOOD.
C'MON, WE'VE GOT TO GET TO MER QUICKLY!
WE HAVE TO WARN THEM THAT THE ATLANTEAN ARMY IS ON ITS WAY!
I JUST HOPE WE AREN'T TOO LATE...
RAAAAAAAHHHH
WHAT'S THAT SOUND?

WOAH.

AAAHHHHH

YIKES.
DOES THIS COUNT AS "TOO LATE"?

WHAT IS...?
THERE'S THE GRAND CHARIOT...

IS THAT--?!

MERMIN!

RAAAAHHHH
LET'S GO!!

CHAPTER
FOUR

IN OUR RESEARCH, WE HAVE FOUND A FEW LOCATIONS...
...GIVING OUT STRANGE SIGNALS.
AND YOU THINK ONE OF THEM COULD BE THIS UNDERWATER CITY...?

LIKE AGENT--er, MISTER BIRD SAID, THERE ARE A FEW POSSIBLE LOCATIONS...
CORRECT, MISTER SMITT.
THIS IS THE SPOT WHERE THE SIGNAL IS STRONGEST.
AND SO THAT IS WHERE WE SHALL VENTURE!
WE'RE GETTING CLOSE!
THE READINGS ARE BECOMING MORE ERRATIC.
RAAAAHHH

!!!!
RAAAHHHHHH

RAH!
AAHHH
WOAH
OOF!
GRAR!!
SHEAHHH
YOW!
WAAAAHHH

VOOOOOOOOOOO
READY CANNON!
FIRE!
AUGH!
VZZ!
SHOOOOM!!
YARGH!
SHHZZZ!

ngh...
VOOOOOO
READY THE SHOT!
STAND ASIDE!

THE MONK SQUAD...?
THE ROYAL FAMILY ARE GIVEN A GREAT POWER OVER THE SEA.
BUT AFTER GENERATIONS OF STUDY AND PRACTICE...
...WE HAVE GAINED A FRACTION OF THAT POWER!
HHHFFFF

WHSH!!
HA!

AROOOO!
THE ATLANTEAN FORCES ARE MORE FORMIDABLE THAN I HAD FORESEEN!
I AM OFF TO BATTLE HAND-TO-HAND! MERMIN! YOU MAN THE GRAND CHARIOT IN MY STEAD!
HUH?!
DAD! NO!! I--
AROOOOOO!!!
I DON'T KNOW HOW TO DRIVE THIS THING!!!

AW, CRUSTACEANS!
THE BEAST HAS GONE BERSERK!
WOOAAAAHH!!
ARROOOOOO
YAAAAA!
O-OKAY...COMMANDING THE GRAND CHARIOT...
"JUST LIKE PSYCHICALLY TALKING TO FISH..."
WAAA
S-SOMETHING I'VE ALWAYS BEEN BAD AT...
RAAAA!
GRAND...CHARIOT...? CAN YOU, uh ...HEAR ME...?
ARROO

N-NOW LISTEN, GRAND CHARIOT!
I AM MERMIN, THE NEXT KING!
NEXT TO RULE THE SEA!!
BRACE YOURSELVES, MEN! IT'S COMING THIS WAY!
GRAND CHARIOT!!
I COMMAND YOU TO HALT!!!

RAAAA
YAAAA
RAAAAA
GHA!!
OOF!
Huh?!
What is that...?
UGH!
KICK!
WHACK!
ARGH!

SIR! MERUS'S BEAST IS GOING WILD!
Hm?
Oh...
YES... SEND IN THE REINFORCEMENTS.
BUT, YOU TWO COME WITH ME...
...I WANT TO GET A CLOSER LOOK AT THIS STRANGE VEHICLE...
YESSIR!

VWOOOOO
WAAAA
RAAAA
Oooo, MAK! I WANNA GET OUT THERE AND FIGHT!

NO WAY.
YOU ARE STAYING RIGHT HERE, YOUNG LADY.
MERMA, YOU'RE CRAZY!
BEING HERE ON MAK'S SHIP IS THE SAFEST SPOT ON THE WHOLE BATTLEFIELD!
DON'T YOU FEEL BAD THAT EVERYONE IS OUT FIGHTING FOR PETE, AND YOU'RE IN HERE DOING NOTHING??
NNNNNOPE!

EVEN MY BROTHER IS OUT THERE...

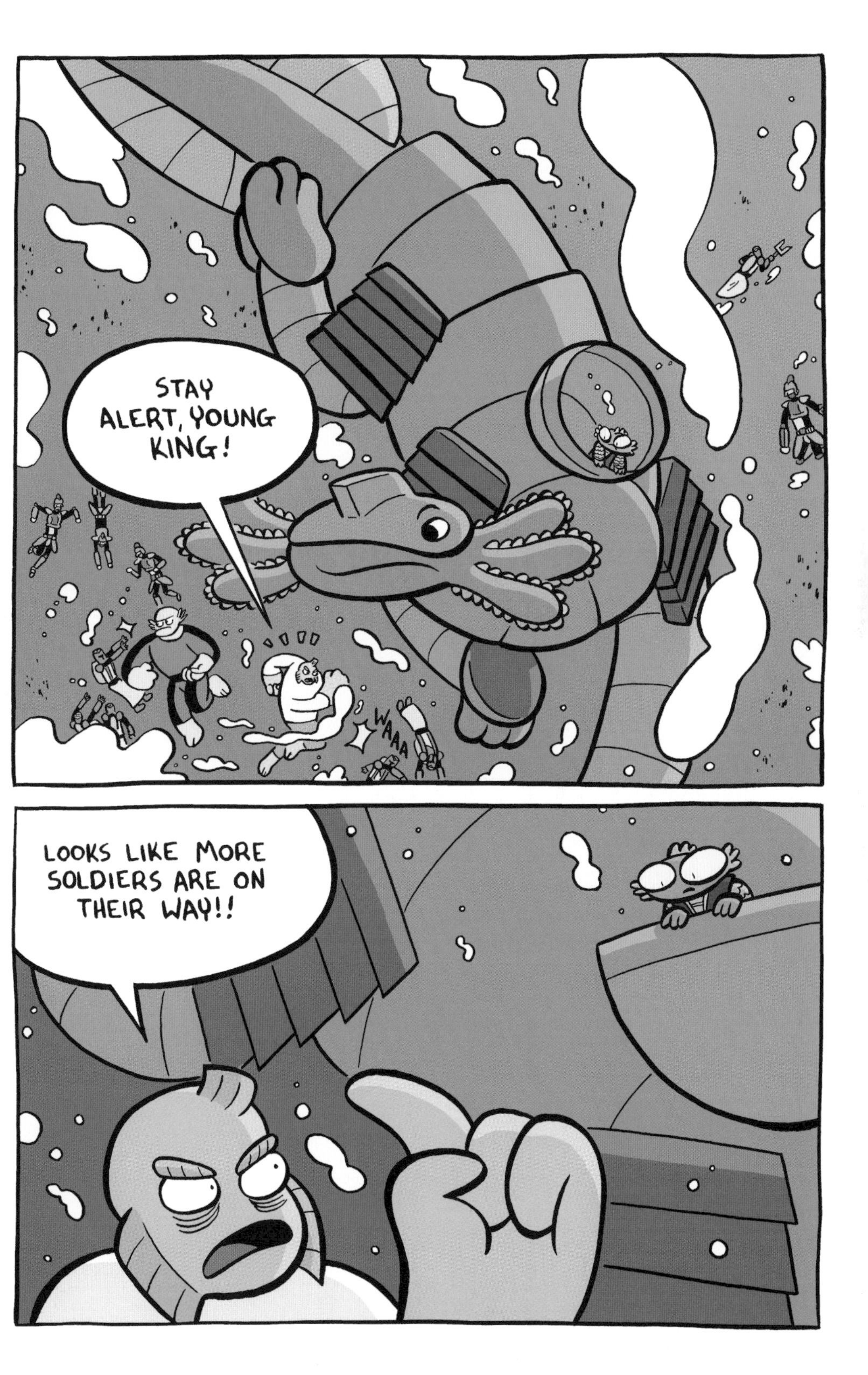
STAY ALERT, YOUNG KING!
WAAAA
LOOKS LIKE MORE SOLDIERS ARE ON THEIR WAY!!

O-OKAY! BE STRONG!
THIS IS NOT WHAT I THOUGHT I'D BE DOING WHEN I WOKE UP TODAY...
HANG IN THERE, PETE!! I'M COMING TO YOUR RESCUE!
I WONDER...
IF COMMANDING THE GRAND CHARIOT IS LIKE TALKING WITH FISH...
F-FORWARD, MEN!
...MAYBE THE SAME GOES FOR TALKING TO HUMANS!
RAAAAHHHHH
IT'S WORTH A SHOT!

OKAY, PETE... IN ATLANTIS, OR WHEREVER YOU ARE...
...CAN YOU HEAR ME? PETE...? PETE??
PETE?!

WOAH!
I CAN SEE HIM!
BUT... WHERE IS HE?
IS THAT... HERE?!?
ON THE BATTLEFIELD?!?

PETE!!
MERMIN?
MERMIN? IS THAT YOU? I CAN HEAR YOU!!
BY THE GREAT DEPTHS, PETE!! I CAN DO IT!!!

MERMIN! YOUR BROTHER--
I KNOW, I KNOW!
MY DAD SAYS THIS IS ABOUT YOU...
...AND ABOUT ENERGEODES...
BUT IT'S JUST ABOUT HOW UPSET HE IS OVER OMER'S DEATH! HE'S OUT OF CONTROL!
N-NO, MERMIN! I MEAN...

SHOOOO
BOOM!
PEAT! WATCH OUT!!
Huh?!?
WHAT'S WRONG?! WHAT WAS THAT?!? PETE?!?

RUMMMBLLE
AAAAAHHHH!!!
OH NO! PEAT!!

DINK!

HM?

OH, PETE!! I'M SO HAPPY TO SEE YOU!
IT'S NOT JUST ME, MERMIN!
LOOK!!

HEY, LITTLE BROTHER.
RIDING THE GRAND CHARIOT NOW, HUH?
...

CHAPTER FIVE

RAAAAA
YAAAAA
TRULY REMARKABLE!

THIS TECHNOLOGY IS PRIMITIVE!
CERTAINLY NOT ATLANTIS-MADE.
HEY! WATCH IT, BUDDY!
MM...
SO, WHAT THAT BOY SAID MUST BE TRUE...
IT... APPEARS SO.
YOU CAN IMAGINE THAT THIS IS UNBELIEVABLE TO US AS WELL!
S-SO, YOU'VE SEEN OUR SON?!

WHERE ARE THE OTHER CHILDREN?!
PRESUMABLY IN MER...
Hmf! REGARDLESS OF THIS DEVELOPMENT, WAR WAS INEVITABLE!
MERUS SEEMS TO HAVE OTHER MAJOR GRIEVANCES!
PLUS, THE CONFLICTS OVER THE ENERGEODE MINES...
INDEED.

Hmm...

OOF!!
RRGH!
WOO-HOO!
GOOD ONE, PENNY!
RAAHH!!!
WOAH!

CLANG
FZZT!
HUH?!
WATCH OUT, TOBY!
CLAIRE?!
RAAAAAAHHHH!
THERE ARE MORE BEHIND US!

RAAAAAAAHHHHHHH
PBTH!
ACK!
SLIP!
YAH!
WHA?!
HA HA! WAY TO GO, BENNI!
WOOAH!!

WHAT ARE YOU DOING HERE?!!
OH!
H-H-HELLO, KING MERUS!

BENNI.
EXPLAIN YOURSELF.
THIS IS NO PLACE FOR CHILDREN.
W-W-WELL, I...uh...
WE MADE HIM TAKE US!
IF IT'S NO PLACE FOR KIDS, THEN WHAT ABOUT MERMIN?
DO NOT CONCERN YOURSELF WITH MERMIN...
...HE IS APTLY ENGAGED IN COMBAT AS WE SPEAK!
RAAAAAA
YAAAAAA

OMER!!!
OOF! HA HA, HEY BUDDY!
I... I THOUGHT YOU WERE...
I'M RIGHT HERE!
AWW!

MERMIN, THIS IS ALEXIS! SHE HELPED US ESCAPE!
WOW! IT'S GREAT TO MEET YOU!!
BUT WHAAAAAAAAAAAT IS THIIIIIIIIIIIIIS...?
SO AWESOME!!

OVER THERE!
RAAAAHHHH
Huh?!
GET BACK, KIDS!
YAAAAAAAAA

YAAAAAHHHH!
VWOO!
RAAA!
WAAA!
RAA
WHAT A MESS.

EVERYWHERE YOU LOOK, IT'S JUST CHAOS...
EVEN--huh?
WHAT IS THAT?
NOT ONE OF OURS, BUT IT DOESN'T LOOK ATLANTEAN...

HOLD TIGHT, KIDS.
I'M GONNA GO GET A CLOSER LOOK AT THIS THING, BUT...I...DON'T...um...
IF YOU'RE LOOKING FOR MERMA, DON'T BOTHER!
SHE LEFT A WHILE AGO!

WHAT?!?
PSH! DON'T WORRY ABOUT HER! GO LOOK AT YOUR MYSTERY SHIP OR WHATEVER...
HA!
RAAAA
WAHHHA

YOU ARE STILL SO MUCH BETTER AT USING POWERS THAN ME!!
PUNCH!
ARGH!
YAAAA!
WAAAA!
WHOOOOOOOOOOSSSHHHH
AW, C'MON BROTHER!
YOU'LL GET THERE WITH PRACTICE!
I GUESS SO...

THIS IS CRAZY.
THE ATLANTEAN KING MET PEAT AND THINKS MER IS BRAINWASHING CHILDREN!
GRR!
VMM!
WHAT?! WELL, DAD IS ATTACKING TO RESCUE PETE FROM ATLANTIS!!
WHOOSH!
YARGH!
THIS IS ALL ABOUT ME?!?
MM...NO... NOT REALLY...
OMER?!?

MERMA! WOW!! EVERYONE'S OUT HERE!
YOU'RE--?! DAD... EVERYONE...WE ALL THOUGHT YOU WERE DEAD!!!
WELL, I'M NOT.
AND SOMETHING HAS TO BE DONE ABOUT THIS MADNESS!

BOTH ARMIES ARE OUT OF CONTROL.
THEY'LL NEVER HEAR US OUT!
I...COULD TRY CALLING OUT PSYCHICALLY...LIKE I DID WITH PETE...
I DON'T KNOW IF I CAN REACH THAT MANY...OR IF THEY'LL LISTEN...
WE NEED TO GRAB THEIR ATTENTION!
THEN ALL THREE OF US HAVE TO DO SOMETHING THEY CAN'T IGNORE!
AW, YEAH!

ALRIGHT! EVERYONE GET BEHIND US!
WSSHH
WSSHH
WWSSHH
WOAH!
RRMMMBLE
OKAY...
READY...
...GO!

WASHO
EVERYONE!

OMM!
STOP THIS FIGHTING!!!

SHAAAHHHH

WAAAHHHHH
OOOOHHHHHH
WSSHHHHH

WOOOAAAAHH!
YAUGH
HOLD TIGHT! THIS IS A BIG ONE!!
ACTIVATE THE CURRENT STABILIZER AT ONCE!!
IS THIS THE END OF "THE DUMPLING"?
THEY DON'T APPEAR TO HAVE THAT TECHNOLOGY!

WHUM!
WE STOPPED! WE SURVIVED!!
THE WAVE IS OVER, BUT HOW DID WE...?

WOAH...
WHAT WAS THAT...?
I'VE NEVER SEEN ANYTHING LIKE IT!
NEITHER HAVE I!
HA HA HA

...WE'RE NOT DEAD!
SIR! THE HUMANS ARE SAFE!
...GOOD... THANK YOU...
HA HA!
WHAT DID WE JUST SEE?!
I KNEW MERS WERE COOL!

WOW, MERMIN! I'M IMPRESSED! YOU HAVE SERIOUSLY IMPROVED!
AW, SHUCKS!
AND MERMA! YOU--
GUYS...?
...ARE YOU...uh, SEEING THIS...?

THE WAVE TORE THE VALLEY FLOOR... AND UNDERNEATH...
ENOUGH ENERGEODES TO POWER BOTH KINGDOMS!
FOR GENERATIONS!
KING MERUS...!
...

I...
...CANNOT BELIEVE MY EYES...
YES! THIS DISCOVERY IS--
NOT THAT!!
...MY CHILDREN!
THEY ARE ALL HERE!!

KING MERUS.
THERE HAS BEEN MUCH CONFLICT BETWEEN OUR PEOPLE.
BUT I BELIEVE IT CAN BE RESOLVED!
Hm. YES. I WENT TO WAR FOR PERSONAL REASONS, BASED ON INCORRECT ASSUMPTIONS.
AS DID WE!
BUT NOW WE ARE ON A CURRENT TO PEACE!
HEAR! HEAR!
clink!

SMITT, THIS PLACE IS INCREDIBLE!
YES! WE'VE MADE A HISTORIC DISCOVERY, MISTER BIRD!
NOW... YOU DO REMEMBER PLEDGING MER'S SECRECY AS WE ENTERED THE KINGDOM...?
uh, oh... YES! YES!
OF COURSE! heh...
achem
MAK! MY FRIEND! DON'T YOU WORRY!
YOU SAVED MY DEAR "DUMPLING," AFTER ALL!

ALL OF YOUR RESEARCH IS ON PAPER, CORRECT?
YES.
YOU CAN'T TRUST DIGITAL!
AND ONLY SINGLE COPIES?
OF COURSE! COPIES COULD FALL INTO THE HANDS OF OUR RIVALS!
INDEED!
NOD
GOOD! GLAD I SHREDDED IT ALL BEFORE THE BANQUET, THEN!
THESE BIGFOOT CHASERS HAVE SUBMITTED SO MANY FALSE CLAIMS IN THE PAST, NO ONE WILL BELIEVE THEM!

WHAT?!?
HA HA! IT'S SO FUN HAVING EVERYONE HERE TOGETHER!!
MY NEW HUMAN FRIENDS AND MY MER FAMILY!

NOW THAT I'M BACK, YOU DON'T HAVE TO WORRY ABOUT RULING THE KINGDOM.
HA HA
Heh... I GUESS I AM A LITTLE DISAPPOINTED ABOUT THAT...
IT WAS PRETTY FUN TO RIDE THE CHARIOT!
AND IF ANYTHING EVER HAPPENS TO OMER, I CAN LEAD MER!

"QUEEN MERMA," HUH? PFFFFF!
I LIKE IT!
WELL, YES...BUT LET'S HOPE OMER STAYS WELL...
HA HA HA
MM-HM!
TRADITIONALLY, ah, THE SONS INHERIT THE THRONE, BUT, ah, I SUPPOSE...
achem!

THE WAR BETWEEN OUR TWO KINGDOMS IS BEHIND US...
YES.
AND I DO SEEM TO HAVE AN ABUNDANCE OF HEIRS...
MERMIN.
I GRANT YOU MY PERMISSION TO RETURN TO DRY LAND.

REALLY, DAD?!!
OF COURSE.
YAY!
AMAZING... I LOVE MER, BUT DRY LAND...?
I DIDN'T EVEN DREAM THAT IT WAS POSSIBLE...!
HA HA
WHAT DO YOU THINK, HONEY?
HOW COULD I SAY, "NO"?
OKAY! MERMIN... ALEXIS... YOU CAN BOTH COME AND LIVE WITH US!
WOAH!
REALLY?!

WOW! THANK YOU ALL,
SO MUCH!!!
MERMIN...
I-I JUST WONDER,
uh, ONE THING...

...CAN I COME TOO?

DON'T MISS THE NEXT BOOK FROM JOEY WEISER...

GHOST HOG

COMING MAY 2019!

Truff is the ghost of a young boar, fueled by fury towards the hunter who shot her down. She has a lot to learn about her new (after)life, and thankfully the forest spirits Claude and Stanley are there to guide her!

However, they soon find that her parents, along with their fellow animal villagers, have been kidnapped by the malicious mountain demon Mava! Truff wants to help, but... the hunter is finally within her grasp, and if she lets him go, she may never get her revenge!

Is vengeance all that being a ghost is good for? Or is there something stronger keeping this little pig tethered to the living world?